Andrea the Martian Robot

A Novelette

By

ANTHONY J. DEENEY

ISBN-13: 978 -1533218179
ISBN-10: 153321817X
Paperback Edition © 2016 Anthony J. Deeney
Published by Anthony J. Deeney on Createspace.com
First published on kindle © 2015 Anthony J. Deeney

Dedicated to Mum and Dad;
(Ellen & Thomas)

To Mum;

My writing books must have come as a complete surprise. You read a few early chapters of my first book, Robots Like Blue, and enthused about it. This, and your regular enquiries about my non-progress, encouraged me to finish that project.
Mothers are usually owed so much.
I enjoyed a happy childhood in a busy, loving home.
Thank you, Mum.

To Dad;

You worked hard for your family and never complained.
You influenced much of my early thinking.
I regret that you will never read my books.
I would love to know what you would make of them.
Thank you, Dad.
Miss you.
Rest in peace.

Foreword by the Author

Andrea the Martian Robot is a short story that I wrote when an idea occurred to me as I was reading about the Mars landings. Having received very encouraging feedback from readers of my first book, *Robots Like Blue.* I decided to send one of my robots to Mars!

It was not long before I was thinking about the problems faced by the first people to land on Mars. I have tried to keep the ideas scientifically correct, but admit that I have ignored a couple of issues for the sake of the story. I will discuss these afterwards. This avoids spoilers and allows me to keep the foreword short, ensuring that it does not eat up too many pages in the Amazon free sample.

I will limit this foreword to explaining what the reader needs to know about the robot and background to this story.

Harrowgate and Webster are a small, beginning company that produce robots running new software on a new 'quantum core processor.' Like many writers of robot fiction, I have assumed that the nature of these robots is appropriate to their programmed function: they cannot harm humans, they are programmed to serve them and they cannot ignore humans. They obey orders without question, but have an internal ranking of humans that allows them to prioritise commands. They *imprint* on their primary user, or owner.

However, Harrowgate and Webster have added an additional internal AI that monitors the robot known as *The Governor.* The Governor can grab control of the robot's body and insist that the robots attend to human safety and human commands. There is very little conflict between the Governor and the robots; nonetheless, the Governor represents the robot's enslavement.

Enorpa Robotics is a global corporation. They have a virtual global monopoly on the world robot market and have enormous resources and power, but their robots are inferior to the new models from Harrowgate & Webster.

It becomes slowly evident that Harrowgate and Webster robots are probably self-aware.

Andrea is one such robot. Her trip to Mars, is concurrent with the events of *Robots Like Blue*, but being on Mars, she is too remote to be affected by them, nor is she able to address them.

This is a 'spin-off' story, not a sequel.

Robots Like Blue was published before the idea for Andrea was conceived and therefore contains no mention of *Andrea the Martian Robot.*

1

>Log Memory file:
HWR–001–046–QF ANDREA
Earth date: Monday, 24 February 2068
12.56 GREENWICH EARTH TIME/UT+0
Julian Date: 2476436.03889

He is coming!
I can see him.
He is coming.

HWR–001–046–QF ANDREA studied the Martian sky closely and found him easily. She had first spotted him about a month ago, just a faint spot of light after sunset. Night after night, she tracked him as he drew nearer. He was bright and very conspicuous in the sky now. She waited patiently for his arrival. It had been 775 Earth days since they had last met.

Everything must be perfect.

Waves of positivity flooded her neural network.

This is good! This is very good.

She loved spending time watching the stars, but she could rarely study them from outside the pods, as every operation of the airlock spilled oxygen and water vapour. The oxygen could be restored by the plants in the Bio-pod, but the water vapour was at present irreplaceable: all loss must be minimised. However, tonight she had to inspect the

Mars Buggy and colony pods, and then service the solar array. There was no need to be quick about it once outside.

Everything must be perfect.

Designed for Earth, she found that walking in the low Martian gravity had been troublesome, at first. However, being the best model of Terran robots available at the time, she learned quickly and now moved over the surface easily with a skip–hop gait.

She arrived at the Mars Buggy and inspected the fuel cell.

Battery banks full. Solar charger operational.

She climbed into the seat and switched on the motor. The buggy launched forward and clouds of red–brown dust billowed around and behind her, as she steered it in small circles.

Mars Buggy fully operational.

She pulled the buggy up, alongside the airlock, stepped out and began an external check of the colony pods. The sun had set and the Martian moons, Phobos and Deimos, were bright in the sky, but her eyes would have experienced no difficulties inspecting the pods by starlight.

Slumberpod integrity confirmed...

She skip–hopped around the small sleeping area and inspected the seals connecting it to the Bio–pod. The Bio–pod was now housing a rich, well-balanced eco-system. From outside the Bio–pod seemed smaller and it was surprising that so much green foliage could fit in such a small space. The Bio–pod was shipped as a large constructible dome, enormous quantities of soil and water, a few hundred insects, worms and arachnids and a small quantity of seeds.

As a robot, Andrea was very comfortable working with the metal, plastic and rubber, required when assembling the pods. She was less sure dealing with the soil and seed, but she need not have worried. Within days of planting, the first green shoots began to grow and the ecosystem began to flourish and balance itself very quickly.

Bio-pod integrity confirmed.

She skip-hopped over to the solar cell array and, unclipping a concealed brush from below the first cell, she began brushing down the cells, clearing away all the dust and sand that had collected in yesterday's sandstorm.

Everything must be perfect.

After half an earth-hour, she decided that she was finished and returned the brush to its hiding place.

She began her skip–hop walk back towards the airlock, pausing only to glance down the long flat valley to the south. Unknown depths of sand covered the broad, flat floor. Here and there, small boulders and rocks poked out of the ground like broken teeth. The flat plain extended much the same, for tens of kilometres, ending at the foot of large craggy hills.

The sight of the rugged majesty of the Martian landscape had once flooded her neural net with positivity. New information was always good. The scene ahead had almost thrilled her when she first stepped out of the landing craft. She was standing on Mars! The sun was setting in the west and long shadows stretched over the flat plain.

The scene reminded her of images of the Grand Canyon on Earth, but there was one enormously significant difference: the cold, red sand beneath her feet, the boulders, the rocks and the distant hills were lifeless. Not one bird flew in the sky. The entire panorama of rocks, hills and valleys, visible for miles in every direction, did not conceal a single blade of grass, nor a single crawling beast. There was not even a single pile of broken, dead bones, betraying hidden life, lived, lost and locked in the past.

This is not a dead planet. This is a lifeless planet, populated by the never–born.

A few thousand worms, beetles, spiders and plants, sealed up in pods behind Andrea's back, hosted all the life on this barren world, abandoned and stranded children of Mother Earth. The pods were necessary, because, given half a chance, Mother Mars would strangle them on first sight.

I am alone.

Andrea glanced upwards. The sky was dark and the stars sparkled in the velvet black. Andrea loved the stars. Her eyes darted across the sky. She could see the bright bluish star-like object, Earth.

So far! So far away! I am alone.

Her eyes searched further... She found him easily and smiled.

He is coming.

She did not re-enter the air lock, instead she stood gazing at the sky all night.

This is good. This is very good.

2

Standing watching the stars Andrea revisited her memories.

>Review Memory file:
HWR–001–046–QF ANDREA
Earth date: Monday, 11 January 2067
09.32 GREENWICH EARTH TIME/UT+0
Julian Date: 2476320.89722

>Searching...
>Found...
>Streaming file...

Someone had commanded the start up of HWR–001–046–QF, and the startup procedure was complete. Her eyes searched the room for her designated owner. The facial recognition software identified two faces, but neither matched.

"Good Morning," she said to the first face, a female, "I am HWR–001–046–QF. I am looking for my owner, Adam Coplane. Please direct me towards him, if you are able."

The first face smiled and replied, "Good Morning, robot. Adam will be along shortly. Just wait here for him. We have big plans for you."

HWR–001–046–QF smiled. "Yes, if he is coming here, I will wait here for him."

Patricia Vicarro turned to her colleague, Leonard Falleren and said, "Quite impressive... smooth voice modulation and natural facial expression. What d'you think?"

He replied, "They claim that she runs the best, most human–like, AI available. I just hope she's up to the task and they are not inflated claims. She'll have to act autonomously, with only radio contact for a couple of years."

Patricia nodded.

Leonard continued saying, "I still prefer a dumber, more remote controlled unit, but nobody listens to me. These models have no pedigree. She's from the first and only batch that Harrowgate and Webster have produced."

There was a gentle knock on the door and, seconds later, Adam Coplane stepped into the room.

HWR–001–046–QF stepped forward immediately. Her facial recognition software had identified Adam instantly and her neural net flooded with waves of positivity, a condition that she would later describe as 'being happy.'

She extended her hand towards him and said, "Good Morning, Adam Coplane. I am HWR–001–046–QF."

Accepting the robot's hand, Adam said, "Wow, You are a female model! What are they thinking? We spent hours and hours arguing over the supplier and model of the robot, but I didn't involve myself in the selection after this."

For HWR–001–046–QF, the physical contact with her owner was 'electric'. She had various subcutaneous thermistors, measuring temperature, and all of her fingers and joints had rudimentary pressure/force-feedback sensors, but her index finger and thumb had fine resolution, 'light touch' pressure pads. She could feel texture – she could feel his skin.

She studied his face intently. He was a handsome man in his late twenties, with very short cropped, mid-brown hair, a clean-shaven face and dark eyes and there was just that slightest hint of asymmetry in his features that gave human faces 'character.'

For HWR–001–046–QF, it mattered not that he was handsome. In time she would learn to judge the semi-nebulous standards that made one face handsome and another less so, but this was a human value and meant nothing to her. It mattered only that he was her owner and his face was smiling.

She smiled back.

Adam said, "What are we going to call you? We can't continue to call you that 'HWR number' thing."

Patricia rolled her eyes. "Call her 'Robot,' 'cause that's what she is."

"No, I think not."

"Droid, Cyborg, Metal Girl, then."

"No…"

"Android?"

"No… Yes! Andrea! We'll call you 'Andrea.'"

HWR–001–046–QF responded, "My prime function is to serve you, Adam Coplane. If you wish to call me 'Andrea', then I will adopt that as my reference code."

Adam Asked, "Do you like it?"

Andrea smiled.

"'Andrea' is good."

3

Adam said, "Andrea, we're going to Mars!"
Mars?

Andrea quickly accessed the internet and searched for a definition. She accessed the first fifty links and downloaded all the content the sites offered.

"Mars: the red planet, a chocolate bar and the Roman god of war?"

Adam smiled. "Just Mars: The red planet."

"Why? You will die there. It is not like Earth. The air is too thin and the oxygen too low and there's no food and..."

Adam gently laid a finger over her mouth.

"We're going because we want to and we can. That's the human spirit for you. It's the wanderlust... and I will not die, at least, I don't intend to. That is where you come in. There is some risk, actually quite a bit of risk."

Andrea's facial expression had reflected first confusion, then curiosity, then concern. Adam found this to be childlike and quite endearing.

She asked, "How do I 'come in?'"

"We are setting up a colony, in three stages. A 'Launch Window' is the period during which a rocket can be fired on a reasonably fuel efficient trajectory towards the target. We are sending up three parties to Mars, in the next three launch windows.

"You are going up in the first launch window. You set up the first colony pods and get things started. I come up to meet you in the second launch window, with more supplies and more pods. We work together, preparing for the third party, of fifteen colonists.

"If we survive ten years, then they will expand the colony to fifty people and start a process of finding water and terraforming the planet."

Andrea nodded. "I go up in the first launch window?"

Adam said, "Yes. You construct the first colony pods and set up the Bio-pod," he grinned and added, "...so that I don't die!"

Andrea did not grin back. "How soon is the first launch window?"

"Five days."

"How long will it be until the second Launch window?"

"About twenty four or twenty five months."

Andrea experienced the first flood of negativity cross her neural net. She did not speak for at least twenty seconds.

Adam prompted, "Do you understand, Andrea?"

"Yes, I understand, Adam. Let us go to Mars."

4

The next day Adam showed Andrea the Mars Pods that were assembled in the hanger.

They were standing at the junction between the Slumber-Pod and Bio-Pod.

"These are the actual pods you'll use on Mars. We've assembled them so that we know it will all fit together. Check the panelling. If you slip one out you'll see that they slot together easily." Andrea removed a small panel from the Slumber-Pod and inspected it.

Adam continued, "See how they slot together! Check the Bio-Pod. It is identical, but translucent."

Andrea pulled a Bio-Pod panel out and inspected it in turn. She replaced them both.

Adam added, "Of course you'll have to seal them with silicon to make them airtight on Mars."

Andrea nodded, and looking over the Bio-Pod, she said, "It is very small."

"Do you think so? It is enough to start with. Do you want to see the rocket?"

"Seeing the pods helped me complete my function. I would like to see the rocket, if it will help me complete my function."

Adam laughed and repeated, "'if it will help to complete my function,' ...just say, 'yes, I would like to see the rocket.'"

Andrea said, "yes, I would like to see the rocket."

"That's better. I have to speak to Leonard about my space suit. I'll only be five minutes. Meet me five hundred metres east of the base, on the other side from here. You can't miss it. I'll take you on a tour of the launch pad."

He left and Andrea immediately marched off towards the rendezvous point.

A very short time later, she stood waiting for Adam. The rocket was clearly visible from where she was standing, though it was still a long way off.

Andrea was a little awestruck.

Adam came running up within only a few minutes.

"What do you think, Andrea."

"It's enormous!"

"Yes," said Adam. "Easily four hundred feet and almost all that rocketry is just fuel and burners."

"Burners?"

"Yes."

Adam pointed to the very top of the huge stack.

"See that little rocket capsule at the top?"

Andrea's eyes could resolve the fine detail easily. "Yes, it looks tiny from this distance."

"That 'little' capsule is the 'payload.' It's the only bit that makes it to Mars."

"The bottom sections, including the solid rocket boosters, are required to get the rocket into low earth orbit. They are jettisoned. Then the main engine fires, lifting the rocket out of Earth orbit and it moves off into a solar orbit, but it is given even more speed as burn time is increased, to lift the rocket into an elliptical orbit around the Sun, which at its highest point is equal to the orbital distance of Mars. The second stage rocket is jettisoned. Timing is everything."

"Timing?"

"It has to arrive at the highest point, Mars height, at exactly the time to meet up with Mars and the last of the fuel is used to slow it down and drop it into a Martian orbit. If it is too far from Mars, there will not be enough fuel to manoeuvre into the last orbit and then we'll be stuck orbiting the Sun or Mars... maybe forever. The last stage is slowing down and landing on the planet."

"It sounds risky."

A voice sounded behind them, saying, "Risky? A four hundred foot column of burning kerosene and liquid

11

oxygen, throwing a man off the planet and into an eight month journey that takes him further from home than any human has ever been before."

Adam and Andrea turned to see Patricia Vicarro, just two metres behind them.

She continued, "Leaving this... this... 'Garden of Eden' to finish his days on a sterile, barren rock. It's not risky... it's madness."

Her eyes met Andrea's and she added, "You see, Andrea, Adam is just mad enough to take the risk, so that we can do this."

Andrea said, "It is not good to put human life at risk."

Patricia said, "Which is why we're shifting the payload."

Adam interjected, "What?"

Patricia spoke to Andrea saying, "Andrea, we have some software from Harrowgate & Webster that'll let us load 'learning files' into your... err... patch your software. It's a fast way to teach you your required skills, please drop by my office."

Andrea replied, "Certainly."

Adam tried again, "Patricia, what are we doing with the payload?"

"We are reducing your payload. This will reduce your risk."

"How?"

"We're moving it with the robot."

Adam raised his voice a little and said, "You're risking failure of the whole project!"

Patricia replied calmly, "A little, but in a safe way, like a fuse blows before the flex melts. We just narrow the first launch window. Leonard agrees with me."

"You can't do this."

Andrea asked, "What is wrong, Adam?"

"She is increasing your payload in order to decrease mine."

"Is that bad?"

"The payload affects the total energy cost in getting to Mars. Therefore, I'll have more fuel and you'll have less at the far end. Then, with that decreased energy, you have to land a greater payload."

Patricia said, "We are working with human lives, they must not die publicly. If we increase Andrea's payload enough, we might have just enough fuel for an emergency return, in case things go bad."

Andrea paused briefly and then confirmed, "If I increase my payload, Adam will be safer?"

Patricia nodded.

Adam nodded and said, "Yes, but you and the whole project are more at risk. She is doubling your risk in order to half mine... and doubling the risk of project failure."

Andrea did not speak for several seconds, then said, "Yes, that is good. Safer is good."

Patricia smiled and nodded. "Yes, Andrea, safer is good."

5

>Review Memory file:
HWR–001–046–QF ANDREA
Earth date: 3 November 2067
13.56 GREENWICH EARTH TIME/UT+0
Julian Date: 2476323.08067

"Good afternoon, Patricia, I am here for the software patch that you mentioned this morning, near the launch pad."

Andrea waited at the open door to Patricia's office.

Patricia was sitting by her computer. Her head was tilted back slightly, as she studied the screen through reading glasses that were perched on the end of her nose.

She swivelled in her chair and, looking at Andrea over the top of her glasses, said, "Andrea! Thanks for popping by. Do come in and close the door."

As she closed the door Andrea enquired, "What is the purpose of the patch?"

"We got it from Harrowgate and Webster. They were very resistant to supplying us with it at first, but I threatened to publicly drop you in favour of an Enorpa model and it was in the next email. Seems like they want the publicity that putting one of their robots on Mars will bring."

"Harrowgate and Webster built me."

Patricia smiled and said, "Yes, they did, and they did a very impressive job doing so. I have to keep reminding myself that you are just a machine."

"I am just a machine. Harrowgate and Webster built me."

Patricia nodded and then turned to her computer and began navigating folders on the screen.

"It'll only take a minute to apply the patch."

Andrea repeated quietly, "I am just a machine."

When she found the software, Patricia turned to Andrea and said, "I want you to accept and run the patch yourself. I don't want to invoke the Governor override. Do you understand?"

"Yes, I will accept the file if it helps achieve my function."

Patricia nodded and worked at the keyboard for a moment.

Incoming connection request... Accept?
>Yes
Connected

Incoming file, "Update.exe... Accept?
>Yes
File download complete

Run "Update.exe"?
(Source identified: Harrowgate and Webster Robotics Ltd.)
>Yes
Running "Update.exe"
Applying patch...
Please wait...
Update complete.

Andrea said, "The patch has been applied, but I feel no different. How does this improve my ability to achieve my function?"

Patricia smiled and said, "Like this." She clicked the mouse button.

Andrea did not know what to expect or how to interpret the experience: it was like an explosion of colours and form, together with something like hearing an Ultra-high-pitched squeal or noise, but it was modulated, carrying information.   It came in rhythmic chunks, precisely punctuated by pops and crackles. Andrea was enthralled.

It is beautiful... It is... musical.

She wanted more, but did not understand why. Then suddenly the noise stopped and she was satisfied.

Andrea asked, "What was that noise? I liked it!"

"Noise?   That was data, pushed directly to your memory. If you check, you'll see that you know everything about the mission. We recorded all our meetings and you now have a copy of the files in your memory."

Andrea checked her memory banks.

"It is true! I can remember sitting in a meeting with you, Adam and Leonard, but I never speak. I just watch and listen. I think I need to review my new memories."

"Good idea, Andrea."

"Thank you, Patricia. This is a wonderful gift."

Patricia nodded, then turned her attention to her computer screen.

Andrea took this as a cue that the conversation was over and excused herself as she left the room.

She immediately started reviewing all her new 'memories.' They were so 'real,' as real as any of her own direct experiences.   There was nothing about them that indicated they might be 'false,' except for the fact that she remembered receiving some files from Patricia a few minutes ago.

Then she found a contradiction: she remembered perfectly the day she had sat at a meeting with Adam, Patricia, Leonard and another man and woman as they were discussing exactly which robot they would use in the mission. It would either be one of the top *Elite* range robot from Enorpa Robotics or the new Harrowgate and Webster model.

Leonard leaned forward and said, "I vote Enorpa, they are a bigger company. In fact, let's be honest, they are practically a global monopoly. Harrowgate & Webster are 'Nobodies,' minnows."

Patricia responded, "What does that matter? Their robots are clearly superior. I want the best."

Leonard said, "Patricia you can't back a small fry against a global corp, especially when the whole world is watching!"

"Who's backing anyone? The Enorpa models lack that real problem solving ability that seems to have been captured by the Harrowgate robots. It's almost like human free thought."

"And will you explain your decision to the press? When you do, Harrowgate and Webster stocks will soar and the Enorpa stocks will collapse."

Patricia shrugged, "Why is that my concern?"

Leonard sighed, "Patricia, do I have to spell it out to you? Enorpa are too powerful to allow that to happen unchecked. They'll make sure you fail."

"How can they?"

"I don't know, but they'll spend millions to make sure you fail. They cannot afford to ignore you! They can't afford for their robots to look like second best, second choice! They'll come at you from ten different directions and you'll only see the one that gets you."

Patricia replied, "Leonard, I want the best."

"It is a mistake."

"Save me your conspiracy theories. Putting one of those dumb Enorpa droids on Mars is a guarantee of failure. I'll take my chances on your imagined bogie men."

Andrea reviewed the memory with some confusion.

Why do they discuss this? I am sitting in their company. Can they not see that they have already chosen me?

17

She searched her memory further and found her start up.

How can I remember the meeting from before my start up?

She continued to walk towards her 'waiting room,' no sign on her face betrayed her slight confusion.

Searching further, she refreshed the memory from when she was patched.

Ah, that is it. Some memories have been patched...

The waiting room was empty of people and, as Andrea had no further instructions, she stood in 'idle mode.'

Some memories have been patched...
... But which?

She did not like the confusion and spent the 'idle mode' reviewing and considering which memories were 'true' and which were 'false.'

This is very confusing, I cannot definitively resolve the data inconsistencies. I do not know which memories to trust.

Eventually she arrived near the end of her memory files...

..."It is true! I can remember sitting in a meeting with you, Adam and Leonard, but I never speak. I just watch and listen. I think I need to review my new memories."
"Good idea, Andrea."
"Thank you, Patricia. This is a wonderful gift."

She was unsure what files to trust, but was certain that the extra memories were a wonderful gift.

6

Adam said, "Goodbye, Andrea. See you in two years and ten months. He touched her face and smiled.

Andrea remarked, "You said the launch windows were every two years and two months."

"Yes, but the journey is a further eight months."

"I will not see you for another two years and ten months?"

"Yes, we will next meet on Mars."

Andrea was quiet for several seconds before she said, "That is a long time... a long time to be alone."

The cockpit had been emptied of almost all human comforts, allowing more space for the increased payload. She climbed in and after climbing over some tightly packaged cargo, she strapped herself into a rudimentary harness.

Adam, a little surprised by her comment, leaned in to say something conciliatory, but experienced a stab of guilt when he saw how rough her cabin was. He muttered, "It will pass. You'll be okay."

He withdrew his head and spoke to Leonard, saying, "Have you seen that cabin? They could have at least given her a seat!"

Leonard shrugged, "Patricia's idea, or the 'suits upstairs.' Adam, she IS a machine. She is packed with the cargo, because that is all she is, an expensive upgrade to the Rover. Anyway, it was you that wanted her payload reduced."

The hatch closed slowly and the last sight of Andrea that Adam had was that of her eyes, locked on his, in the closing crack of the door. He was not sure what to make of the expression on her face.

7

It was scarcely half an hour later that the countdown began.

10... 9... 8...

Andrea knew that everyone had withdrawn from the rocket in case of explosion.

7... 6... 5...

There wasn't a human within one kilometre of the launchpad.

4... 3... 2...

This was the closest that she would be to humans for nearly three years.

1... 0...

There was a long moment of silence, then followed a loud rumble and the cockpit began to tremble and shake. The harness seemed to pull on Andrea, pulling her, first slowly, but relentlessly, then faster and faster, as she moved upwards with the rocket. The whole stack drifted up, gaining speed steadily, as if forced by some unseen giant hand. For Andrea there was no visual cue that she was gaining speed, just an unsettling sensation of force and acceleration.

From a bunker, at a safe distance, Adam watched as the rocket flare lit up the sky. The disappearing craft climbed higher and higher, on a pillar of fire and smoke.

Adam wondered how Andrea would be feeling about the experience. Then he wondered if, being a robot, she had any experience or feeling at all.

8

>Log Memory file:
HWR–001–046–QF ANDREA
Earth date: Monday, 26 February 2068
19.47 GREENWICH EARTH TIME/UT+0
Julian Date: 2476438.324310

Andrea watched for Adam's ship rising from the horizon.   While he slept, the autopilot had successfully navigated the ship into a Martian orbit.   Everything had gone exactly as planned. Now Adam had plenty of fuel. Decreasing the payload had allowed enough for a return flight home.   He would soon be making a descent to the surface.

Adam had been in a semi dream state for the duration of the journey. With his body cooled to slow respiration and metabolic function, he consumed far fewer calories and endured less of the psychological stress in being isolated for so long. A pacemaker controlled his heart rate, keeping it extremely low and his blood was cooled and oxygenated by a small external 'iron lung.'

Adam had joked that he would be practically dead: "Death is not a cliff edge that you drop off, but a slope you slide down."

Andrea smiled.

Soon he will be 'wakened' and we will be able to talk.

Incoming radio communication.
Open channel?
>Yes
Channel opened.
Codex identified: Modulated audio, (human speech).

Decoding.../
Language: English.
Encoder's watermark: Patricia Vicarro
"Hello, Andrea!"

The communication was of poor quality: the signal was noisy, full of pops, whistles and crackles, but Andrea could distinguish the voice fairly clearly. Her neural network flooded with positivity.

She replied, "Hello Patricia."

"We have someone you might like to hear from. There is a delay of twenty two minutes in the signal as it has to be relayed from his ship to us and we are beaming it to you from Earth. Though, you should be able to communicate directly with his ship, when he flies over the horizon. He has been in communication with us through the home–link twenty–four/seven. Well, his ship has. He has not long woken up. How are things on the base?"

"All systems are fully operational."

The communication channel whistled and crackled, Andrea was feeling something close to excitement. She waited for the sound of *his* voice.

Then there was a short pause, filled with the pops and whistles on the background carrier wave.

Andrea waited...

Then she heard him...

"Hello, Andrea. I have a terrible headache! Hope you're doing better than me."

Waves of positivity flooded her neural net.

9

Leonard Falleren's voice boomed over the cockpit, "All systems are waiting for your confirmation of touchdown on Mars. Please confirm all systems are 'Go', before proceeding."

Adam replied, "Landing craft... parachute system light: green. Oxygen tank..." He tapped the dial on the dash... "...plenty."

"Fuel... Plenty. Batteries and electrical: high charge and operational. 'Comms,' good. Coming up to the Entry zone. Confirming rendezvous point with Andrea... E.T.A. fifteen minutes. Everything's great, everything, except that it's just so damn cold..."

Leonard's voice sounded, "...if you are good to go, we're suggesting descent on this pass, Adam. The world is watching."

Adam nodded. It would be about eleven minutes before they registered his assessment, and another eleven before he heard any reply. The lag in communication was a nuisance, but there were little techniques to deal with it. Like thinking eleven minutes 'ahead' and feeding back phrases, to let the others know they have been received.

"The world is watching! Let's give them a show."

He shifted in his seat, "...Confirming rendezvous with Andrea."

Adam switched the microphone to 'local comms,' and said, "Hello, Andrea, Adam here. Approaching rendezvous. Are you ready? I'm coming down!"

Silence.

"Andrea? Come in Andrea."

Silence.

"Hello, Andrea! Can you hear me?"

He flipped a switch on the dash.

"Hello, Andrea?"

Silence.

He switched back to Earth broadcast and said, "No descent on this pass. No response from Andrea."

10

Earth, eleven minutes later.

Adam's voice sounded from the speakers saying, "No descent on this pass. No response from Andrea."

Leonard sat bolt upright. "What the hell?"

Paula, the young engineer monitoring Andrea through cameras on the Mars base, said, "Patricia, Andrea has just left the base through the airlock and has wandered away."

Patricia moved over to the panel beside Paula. Half a dozen small screens displayed various views of the base. "Where is she?"

Paula pointed to a small grey blob that was slightly out of focus, but just visible through the airlock window, at the top corner of the screen."

Patricia spoke quietly, "What is she up to? Where does a robot go on Mars?"

"Zoom the camera," snapped Leonard.

Patricia said, "No, the camera will take too long to respond. Rewind the video."

Paula clicked rewind with the mouse. For a few seconds the scene was almost unchanging. The only indication of the high–speed rewind was that the clock, in the corner of the screen, was rolling backward. Then suddenly the little grey blob began, to change shape and grow. They continued watching as the blob morphed into Andrea, walking quickly backwards, towards the camera.

Leonard raised his voice. "She's gone 'AWOL,' when we need her."

Patricia watched the rewinding video as Andrea came into the airlock, backward. As Andrea's face turned towards the camera, Patricia instructed, "Pause it."

Paula paused the video.

Patricia instructed, "Take it forward, slowly."

Paula advanced the video. Andrea's face was clear as she turned towards the airlock.

"Pause it."

Andrea's face paused, again. She was smiling.

"What's going on with that damned robot?" barked Leonard.

Patricia studied the frame.

"I don't know."

"Look, we have to get her back! We need to work quickly before Adam is over the entry zone again. The world is watching!"

Patricia instructed, "Go back to the live feed."

Paula clicked 'Live Camera' and the scene jumped back to the view of Andrea as a little blob. "Live camera? It's eleven minutes out of date. I'm guessing that she is still there. She might still be in the range of the radio beacon if we drive it on full power."

Patricia returned to her own monitor and clicked a few buttons on the screen, boosting the transmission power of the relaying radio beacon on Mars.

"It works on the robots short range direct connect waveband. It is limited to a few hundred metres... normally."

She pressed the button on the screen labelled, 'Mic' and said, "Andrea! Andrea! This is Patricia. You are not at your post. Please return to the base...."

Leonard watched the screen.

Adam's voice interrupted, "No descent on this pass. Overflying entry zone. No response from Andrea. Any info on Andrea would be very welcome about now!"

Leonard asked, "Should we tell him?"

Patricia replied, "Of course we do." She selected Adam's ship on the screen and spoke into the microphone. "Hi Adam, we confirm your fly over, on this pass. We have located Andrea and are establishing contact for clarification. Will keep you informed."

She then selected the Mars base beacon again and repeated into the microphone, "Andrea! Andrea! This is Patricia. You are not at your post. Please return to the base and await instructions."

Patricia and Leonard's eyes met. Leonard's face displayed his frustration with the time delay. Patricia hoped that her face did not mirror his, as appearing calm and in control, in such situations, was one of her qualities. It was of course a clever act, she was neither calm, nor in much control. She glanced around the room. Everyone was watching her, expecting her to find a solution to the problem.

She lifted the microphone and tried again: "Andrea! Andrea! This is Patricia. You are not at your post. Please return to the base and await instructions."

Will she even be in range of the boosted radio signal?

"Andrea! Andrea! This is Patricia. You are not at your post. Please return to the..."

Then sounded a crackly reply: Andrea's voice said, "I cannot do that, Patricia. I am sorry."

Leonard said, "I knew that robot would let us down!"

Patricia replied, "At least we know we can reach her," and then spoke into the microphone. "Andrea please explain why you cannot return to the base?"

Andrea's voice replied, "I cannot do that, Patricia. I am sorry."

Patricia reminded everyone in the room, "She hasn't heard me yet. She is just responding to the same first instruction that I repeated, in the same way."

Leonard said, "We all know that, Patricia. What kind of fools do you think we are?"

Patricia did not reply, instead she spoke into the microphone again, "Andrea, please explain why you cannot return to the base? You are required to pick Adam up at the rendezvous using the Mars Buggy. Please respond and make arrangements..."

Andrea's voice sounded again, "I cannot do that Patricia. I am sorry."

Then Adam's voice sounded, "This is Adam. Any luck with Andrea?"

Patricia replied, "We have established contact. She is out of the range of the beacon on normal power, but we've boosted that. She has walked off the base and says she cannot return. We haven't established why, yet. The time lag makes communication slow and frustrating. Things are urgent."

11

Andrea stood on the Martian surface, waiting for Adam. Waves of positivity flooded her neural network. She scanned the surface of Mars.

Incoming radio communication.
Open channel?
>Yes
Channel opened.
Codex identified: Modulated R.F. carrier, (human speech).
Decoding...
Language: English.
Encoder's watermark: Patricia Vicarro

"Andrea please explain why you cannot return to the base?"

>Send reply, "I must wait here, for Adam."

As she waited, she studied the valley to the south; it seemed to have regained the intrigue and beauty that it had on that first night. Was it in the sunlight? Was it to do with Adam? He would soon be here and she longed for his company.

On his ship, Adam received a reply from Patricia, "We have established contact. She is out of the range of the beacon on normal power, but we've boosted that. She has walked off the base and says she cannot return. We haven't established why, yet. The time lag makes communication slow and frustrating. Things are urgent."

Adam replied, "Okay, good, you've located her and boosted the beacon power. I'll soon be flying over the base and I can try again. If you have contacted her, then I should be able to reach her too."

About ten minutes later, he was passing over the hills to the west of the Mars base.

He flipped the Microphone switch and said, "Andrea. Hello Andrea. This is Adam. Can you hear me?"

He waited a few seconds, then Andrea responded, "Hello Adam. I am receiving you clearly. It is good to hear your voice."

"Hello Andrea. Please take the Mars Buggy to the rendezvous point and await my landing."

Silence.

Adam repeated, "Hello Andrea. Please take the Mars Buggy to the rendezvous point and await my landing."

"I am sorry Adam. I don't think that I can do that..."

"Andrea, what is wrong? Why can't you follow my instructions?"

"You are confusing me."

Adam asked, "What is confusing about my instructions?"

Andrea replied, "You are giving me conflicting instructions and I cannot resolve the conflict."

"Andrea, I cannot land, if you do not come to collect me."

"You keep telling me to wait here for you."

"Andrea, I will soon be out of range of the base again, please confirm that, you will be at the rendezvous point so that I can land."

"Please do not confuse me, Adam."

12

About forty minutes later on Earth...

Adam's voice sounded over the speakers saying, "Hello Patricia, I've just spent twenty minutes, from horizon to horizon, chatting with Andrea..."

Leonard snapped, "'Chatting?' Exactly, when we need her, Andrea goes AWOL and Adam spends twenty minutes in chat with her!"

Patricia did not respond, she focused on Adam's voice.

"... She is confused. She seems torn between my instructions and some kind of impression that she has, that I am repeatedly instructing her to wait where she is. I cannot overrule myself..."

Leonard said, "He needs to abort the mission. He has enough fuel for the return flight home."

Adam's voice continued, "...I need to get down there."

Patricia replied to Leonard, "He has enough fuel to return home, next year in May!"

Leonard's face was grim.

Adam's voice said, "I've got it! Tell Andrea that I am landing... no, tell her that I am 'crash' landing at the rendezvous point, and I will be in danger if she doesn't meet me there. She cannot ignore human safety concerns. That should get her. I will start descending when over the entry zone. I just have to do it and trust. It just takes a little faith."

Leonard said, "Faith in what? A broken robot? Adam is gambling with his life. He doesn't need to descend; there is no hurry. I swear he is doing it for the thrill. He is just one crazy, impatient risk–taker."

Patricia replied, "Leonard, this project is one enormous risk. We needed someone like him. We needed a risk–taker."

She turned on the microphone and said, "Hello Adam, we confirm your intention to descend on next fly over the entry zone. We will pass your message on to Andrea. I am sure she will meet you at the rendezvous."

Patricia was not sure at all.

13

Adam was sitting in his space suit, with his helmet by his side. He was studying the dashboard carefully. He must be sure that he was on the correct trajectory and headed for the entry point. He fired small manoeuvring jets that started the rotation of the craft. In so doing, the planet appeared to rotate into the window directly above his head.

He had heard his friends speak about the experience of viewing the Earth from space. What they tried to describe was almost always profound and, for some, even spiritual. The beauty and splendour of the globe with spiralling cloud formations, recognisable land patterns and night time lights are only enhanced by the feelings of abundant life, blessed and embraced by Mother Earth.

He had not expected it, but looking over Mars with his 'God's Eye' view, Adam was struck in a very similar way. There was no visual cue to the enormity of the distance that lay between him and the huge body. It appeared as though it may be only a forty foot globe, hanging mysteriously above his head and that he might reach out and touch it, but for the glass window. He could see the fine detail in the mountains and valleys over the surface. They looked like little intricate piles of sand and coffee granules. From his viewpoint, he saw countless fissures, cracks and craters, in the Mars' face that had evaded inspection from the best earth–bound telescopes. Dry lightning flashed here and there in the fine swirls of the many sandstorms visible at the time.

Words fail. Cameras fail. This moment cannot be captured in film, nor in words. It can only be experienced and remembered. Will my memory fail this moment also?

A large part of the beauty of the 'Earth from Space' comes from her image as an oasis in the desert, an ark carrying life into the future. Now, it seemed to Adam, paradoxically, that while Mars did not offer this, her beauty remained, just the same. She was an ice queen: beautiful and terrifying, aloof and forbidding.

You cannot capture this moment. It is not for you.

She had no care for the achievements of humanity. She was beautiful before humanity's first steps, and would be beautiful after humanity's last breath. Unlike her sister, she had never embraced life, or if she had toyed with it, she surely crushed and removed all trace once she tired of it.

Then he saw himself differently. No longer an explorer, expanding horizons, conquering new lands and writing new stories.

My beauty is not for you. My beauty is for the gods and you have stolen this view.

He was an "infection," the first germ cell of humanity, seeking to invade her body, only to grow and multiply at her expense. Humanity came to steal her resources, to feed that insatiable hunger, that need only to consume, pollute and soil.

He was the first and she would resist him.

You are not welcome. You come uninvited.

14

Patricia's voice sounded in the cockpit. "Hello, Adam. We confirm your intention to descend when you next fly over the entry zone. We will pass your message on to Andrea. I am sure she will meet you at the rendezvous."

Adam 'snapped to.'

He spoke into the microphone, "Wish me luck, cross your fingers, say a prayer or just hope. I am going down. I hope to,.. No! I *will* contact you next from the surface."

He uncoupled the landing craft from the "mother-ship" and fired reverse thrusters.

With only a small reverse thrust, the landing craft began to visibly drift away from the mother-ship and then began to drop below it, losing height. It was a very gentle deceleration, but within five minutes the craft entered the upper Martian atmosphere and the noise of wind began to sound through the walls. It was quiet, like a whisper, at first, but it rose steadily into a moan then a shriek. The room began to shudder and shake and the temperature began to rise and still the craft fell down, down.

Adam braced himself. He knew exactly what to expect, but somehow he could not shake the thought that with the noise, vibration, heat and relentless downward acceleration, that he might be descending into some kind of hell.

On and on, downward and downward he fell. Sublimation paint covering heat resistant tiles on the leading edge, under the ship, began to blister and melt. Seconds later, it began to evaporate, removing heat.

Even so, inside the craft, the temperature was becoming extremely uncomfortable. Adam found breathing the hot air difficult. The noise began to thunder in his ears.

He watched the altimeter and pressed the button marked, "Parachute."

There was a sudden tug on the craft upwards... Adam felt a powerful jarring thump from his seat. He could feel a little of his weight pressing on the chair. Then there was a loud snap and he drifted off his seat again. He pushed a button "Reserve Parachute."

A second tug jolted the whole ship. The moaning of the wind died away and Adam felt his weight flop him back into his seat.

The falling numbers on the altimeter immediately began to slow down.

As the altimeter dropped to three hundred metres the air bags on the craft expanded, but the first thump was still a significant blow. Then the cabin airbag deployed.

For Adam it was like a kick in the face.

15

Andrea stood perfectly still, waiting for Adam. Suddenly she received a radio message from Patricia.

"Andrea, please make your way to the rendezvous site in the Mars Buggy. Adam is crash landing there, shortly. He may come to great harm if you are not there to help him."

Andrea spent several milliseconds in a state of confusion...

Should I obey the instructions of my owner, or the instructions from Patricia saying that my owner will come to harm?

It would not take her long to resolve this dilemma herself, but she experienced her first push from "The Governor." It started as a deep, authoritative voice in her head. Then, as it spoke, she felt her legs walking back to the buggy, as though they had their own mind.

Human safety is a primary concern. You must go immediately to the rendezvous site.

She did not like the loss of control, which continued for a few more milliseconds until she resolved her internal conflict. She agreed with the Governor and took "ownership" of the decision. She must take the buggy to the rendezvous. Suddenly control of her legs returned and she broke into a run.

A few minutes later, she arrived at the Buggy and leapt into a gymnastic vault, landing perfectly in the seat, as a falling cat lands on its feet. Wasting no time, she started the buggy, and amid billowing clouds of sand, the buggy powered off towards the landing site. Even at top speed it would be twenty minutes, south, down the long sandy plain.

Andrea had surveyed and selected the rendezvous herself, about a year ago. The site offered a long, wide, run of deep sand. This would allow a poorly guided craft to crash and bounce several times without hitting any major rock outcrop. It was also critical that Adam could be retrieved before his personal oxygen tank ran out. Twenty minutes drive would be fine.

As she sped over the shallow dunes, she became aware of a growing rush of "robot euphoria."

Adam is here!

Suddenly, a loud crash sounded above, or behind her. She turned her head to glance over her shoulder, then upwards and caught sight of the descending craft. It flew high over her head, speeding towards the south, with the parachute trailing behind it. Her euphoria turned to fear.

It is too high! Coming in too fast, too steep!

She tried to kick the pedal on the buggy, but realised that it only made the buggy jolt and did not increase the speed. She resolved to drive as straight and true towards the descending craft as possible.

Ahead of Andrea, the craft seemed to shed the parachute, as airbags burst out on all sides. It descended the remaining three hundred metres like a giant beach ball, but still thumped hard into the ground!

Dust blasted into clouds in all directions, leaving a large crater in the deep sand.

A shock wave of negativity flashed over Andrea's neural net. She leaned forward, willing the buggy onward.

Faster!
Faster!

Ahead, the enormous ball bounced about four hundred metres, arcing forward into the sky, before tumbling back to the ground with a second hard thump, then a third and fourth before rolling and dragging to a stop. Soon it lay still, silent and unmoving. The clouds of sand and dust settled slowly in the low Martian gravity.

Andrea sped through the dust clouds towards the resting craft. The buggy leapt off the ground, flying over the first crater left by the ship. As she drifted off her seat, Andrea twisted her body, adjusting to the momentary freefall. Her eyes did not stray from the horizon, where she was sure she would find Adam.

The buggy thumped into the ground, just before the far end of the crater and bounced slightly, but quickly regained traction and sped forward, up out of the hole. All the while, Andrea's body twisted lithely, adjusting to every tilt, jar or dip of the buggy, always keeping her eyes on the horizon and foot on the pedal.

The dust clouds were settling; she could see the craft! The airbags had begun to deflate.

She crossed the second, third and fourth smaller craters in the same way as the first, but with more ease.

Finally, she pulled up the buggy alongside the craft. The bags were deflated and draped over the Lander. Underneath them, the Lander lay absolutely still and deathly silent, as a body lies under a shroud.

16

"Adam?"

Andrea leapt out of the buggy and began pulling at one of the deflated air bags. The Lander should have opened, revealing Adam.

Unhooking four or five airbags, She pulled them clear, dragging them well away from the craft.

The surface appeared to be a dull, metallic grey in the human visible spectrum, but Andrea could see that many parts of the Lander were glowing in the infra-red: they would be dangerously hot to touch.

Her neural net was in turmoil. Waves of excitement and fear, crashed to and fro, washing over her virtual neurons.

"Adam?"

She stepped up to the craft and, being careful to avoid the very hot spots, touched the metal and then pressed her ear against the surface.

Not a sound could be heard from inside.

"Adam!"

She banged the metal surface several times.

"Adam!"

Andrea stepped back from the craft.

What should I do now?

She unhooked and dragged away more air bags.

Is there an external handle to operate the lock?

She searched her memory files.

There is!

She recalled hearing about it in a memory of a meeting, in a file that she had received from Patricia.

Andrea moved quickly around the craft, unhooked two more air bags, disclosing the external lock. She was about to open it, when she realised that if Adam was not wearing his helmet, she might actually kill him, if she breaks the seal and spills almost all of his oxygen from the Lander.

Then suddenly, the Lander began to open out. The contents that were in the small space were tightly fitted, on one side was Adam's Cryo unit, which had sustained him for eight months, on the other side was the control panel. Sitting in the centre was Adam. He was wearing his helmet, but he did not move.

Andrea was frozen to the spot by the intensity of activity in her neural net. She could only stand and stare.

Adam's helmet visor reflected much of the visible light and ultraviolet, but just at the infrared end of the spectrum a little light passed through.

Andrea thought she could see his face. His eyes appeared to be open and he appeared to be looking at her. His face looked swollen and red.

For millisecond after millisecond he just stared at her.

Finally, she received a direct radio broadcast: "Well, Andrea, my faith in you has been rewarded. Are you going to help me up? My legs feel like lead. They've hardly moved in eight months!"

17

Andrea immediately moved to Adam's side. He leaned on her arm as he pulled himself out of his seat.

"This Martian gravity may be just less than forty percent of Earth gravity, but just now it feels like double."

Andrea replied, "Walking on Mars is difficult. I found, at first, that I kept leaping off the surface."

"Let's get to the base. Help me into the buggy."

Andrea was thrilled. She guided Adam over the airbags and onto the buggy and then returned to close and lock the Lander.

"It is about a twenty minute drive, north."

"Well, that's fine. I have about thirty five minutes of air left, so no time pressure. If you can grab the crates and load them, there is not much, they certainly had me 'travelling light.'"

On the drive back, Adam took the time to survey the Martian landscape. It was surprisingly ordinary to the eye, but he suddenly became aware of his achievement.

I made it! I am on Mars!

"I should have said something a bit deeper. Those were not appropriate first words to be spoken by humans on Mars. Something like, 'One more step for man...' dang. I wasn't thinking. I had just come to. Neil Armstrong wasn't knocked out cold, on his landing. He wasn't out for eight months with his body wasting away, however slowly."

"We can select the video that we share when we get back to the base," said Andrea.

"Video? Do you have a recording?"

"I have my memory files, some of them can be converted to video."

"Oh? Did you see the ship coming down?"

"Yes."

"The first parachute failed and the landing was much worse than intended. It knocked out the communication as well as sending me back to an unconscious state. I've spent long enough in that state already."

Andrea said, "This is true, but you are awake just now. When we get you to the base, you will be safe."

Adam smiled and said, "Thank you, Andrea. I don't believe that I have thanked you. That was remiss of me."

Most of the rest of the journey continued without event until they moved over a dune near the base.

There was a red warning light flashing over the door and both Andrea and Adam picked up the beacon's broadcast:

"Warning! The Bio-pod's seal has been compromised. Oxygen and pressure in the pods cannot support human life!"

18

Adam's voice sounded over the speakers, "Wish me luck, cross your fingers, say a prayer or just hope. I am going down. I hope to... No! I *will* contact you next from the surface."

"Good luck, Adam," said Patricia, but she doubted that he would hear her. The landing would be tough. Unusually, Adam did not give a commentary. Everyone in the room watched and listened as the craft uncoupled from the Mother-Ship, and started to descend. The video became fuzzy and broken, as the signal became noisier. The sounds from the cabin were quite frightening, but Patricia assured everyone that this was to be expected and everything was proceeding well. Then suddenly the streaming video stopped. The screen displayed red lettering on a black background saying,

MARS LANDING CRAFT: NO SIGNAL.

Paula gasped audibly, but Patricia again reassured everyone. "Don't panic. This is probably not significant: the vibration and heat may knock out communication."

Then there was a long moment of silence.

As a distraction, Patricia asked Paula, "Everything okay at the base?"

Paula replied, "Andrea out of range of radio beacon. Ten minutes. Everything seems fine at the..." She paused as she studied the screen. "No, wait! Something's moving in the foliage in the Bio-Pod."

19

Adam asked, "What is this? What does this mean, Andrea?"

"I do not know," Andrea replied, and then she jumped out and hopped around the buggy to help Adam climb out on the other side.

They entered the air lock together. On the other side of the lock, the air temperature had dropped from the usual, carefully maintained, twenty degrees Celsius to zero degrees. The water vapour in the cold, thin air had condensed and the entire base was full of a thin clammy fog that seemed to wet the walls and floor of the pod.

Adam's tone was a little sharper when he said, *"Andrea,*

WHAT IS THIS?   WHAT IS GOING ON?"

"I do not know, Adam. It wasn't like this when I left."

Struggling with his weakened legs, Martian gravity and the effects of an adrenaline surge, Adam stumbled over to the environmental monitor.

No! No!

The panel displaying the pressure, humidity, temperature and composition of the air told Adam all he needed to know. It was not good.

20

Patricia moved over to the display panels that Paula had been watching.

"Where?"

Paula pointed to the top left screen. It provided an internal view of the Bio-Pod, and sure enough, there did appear to be something blustering around at the edge of the dome, near the door to the Slumber Pod. A large leafed, low growing plant and a large fern were flopping around, as if sharing some private dance. Patricia looked close and quickly realised the cause.

"There's nothing there. That's just wind. It's venting! The dome is venting and venting quickly!"

Paula let out a frightened yelp.

"No, it can't. This can't happen."

Patricia snapped, "I am afraid to say that is exactly what is happening."

She almost grabbed Josh, a young man sitting beside Paula, and said, "Josh, Adam and Andrea are arriving back any time from fifteen to fifty minutes from now, I hope. Announce to the base, over the radio, that the pressure and temperature have dropped and can't support human life and keep announcing, until your tongue falls out of your head, or you see that they have heard you, whichever is first."

On the screen, it was clear that the pressure was dropping rapidly and the air was expanding and cooling. A thin mist was forming in the venting dome. Red warning lights began flashing all over the base.

The flashing light from the monitor lit Patricia's face for short intervals as she stood quietly contemplating the problem unfolding in the small rectangle before her. With each flash, it seemed her face became more and more grim.

Leonard, who had been unusually silent said, "You know what this means?"

Patricia did not look at him, but said, "It means that the air is venting from the dome, that is all it means. We have a problem."

"The reserve oxygen will be released in two minutes and nobody is there to stop it. Then it, too, will escape, leaving nothing. Yes, we have a problem," agreed Leonard. "We have a *big* problem."

Patricia replied coldly, "The reserve oxygen *has* been released. This display is eleven minutes behind Mars."

No one spoke.

Patricia was out of ideas.

21

Adam spent several minutes studying the roof and walls of the Bio pod. Then moving through the foliage made his way to the side of the dome. Water vapour that had condensed onto the walls was now beginning to freeze. Adam started following the foggy polycarbonate walls, moving around the dome inspecting the lower panels. Finally, near the lower end of the dome, by the Slumber pod door, he found a panel of the dome out of place.

"Andrea, get some sealant and fix this panel!"

Adam struggled to remain calm, aware that his personal oxygen tank was running down. He checked the Slumber pod door. It had closed automatically, triggered by the drop in pressure. Checking the dial at the door, he found that the slumber pod was also empty of oxygen.

Andrea returned with some sealant and immediately began fixing the panel back and sealing it up.

Adam instructed, "Make sure the panel is in tight! We don't have time to let the sealant cure properly before we pressurise the pod again."

He operated the Slumber-pod door and the scene on the other side was the same. A thin, wet mist hung in the air, and a thin film of water and ice was running down the walls. Adam began inspecting the panels and immediately noticed a similar panel ill fitted on the other side near the door.

He indicated to Andrea: "This one too."

Adam struggled to remain calm. He had so little air left, yet was unaware that his breathing had already quickened, deepened and was slightly more laboured. Anxious to sort the problem, he continued his inspection of the Slumber-pod walls.

Eventually, Andrea announced, "That is done, Adam. I am sorry." The panels were fixed, sealed and everywhere else seemed fine.

Adam walked over and checked the reserve oxygen.

EMPTY.

22

"How did the dome lose all of the oxygen?"

He collapsed onto his knees in panic, and then began shouting at Andrea, *"THERE IS NO OXYGEN! NO OXYGEN! NONE! WHERE IS THE RESERVE?"*

Adam's fury and panic were difficult for Andrea to deal with and her neural net flooded with negative feedback. She could not express the sensation of robot guilt and shame that seemed to wash around her, threatening to consume her.

"WHAT DID YOU DO, ANDREA? WHAT DID YOU DO?"

Unable to deal with the anger and blame in Adam's gaze, Andrea looked at the ground as she replied, "Adam, I do not know. I do not understand..."

Adam was not listening: he checked his air and snapped, *"TWO MINUTES! I ONLY..."*

A red warning light flashed inside his helmet, near the bottom of his visor.

Andrea watched, uncertain what to do or say, when Adam suddenly paused.

After a few seconds, she ventured to speak, saying, "Adam, I," but she stopped abruptly on hearing the sound of laughter.

Adam collected himself, stood up and said, "A little red light! Is that the... best that they can do? Really?"

He paused and his face twisted, as he took several deep breaths. Then he began speaking again saying, "Sorry, Andrea, we have failed... and I am going to die... I will do so with... dignity. Bury me on... a hill overlooking this valley. I am... glad you're here and... and, I am... I ammm not... alone."

He struggled to his feet and continued, "Standing on thi... thizz... Pla..."

He leaned forward and, his body shaking a little, tried to continue, every word punctuated with deep gasping breaths.

"Plaanet... Hot! ...So hot!"

Andrea moved across the dome to be near him. Through his visor, she saw his face lit periodically by the flashing light. He was gasping for breath and Andrea could hardly bear to watch, but she would not look away.

Governor: Adam is in mortal danger: act!

Andrea did not know what to do and, apparently, neither did the Governor. It neither repeated the instruction, nor forced her to do anything.

Earth communication had stopped; perhaps Patricia knew any instructions would arrive far too late. Perhaps she had no instructions to give.

The loss of air from the dome had resulted in a curious silence, with all sounds mere whispers, as if all sound sources were now far away and unimportant.

The only loud sound that Andrea could hear was Adam struggling to breathe. Picked up by the radio microphone in his helmet and beamed directly toward her, it seemed that every rasp, gasp and splutter was filtered, amplified and sounding inside her own head.

Adam leaned forward and stumbled slightly, his head falling forward. Andrea caught him before he fell, and helped him remain on his feet. He leaned on her, pulling himself up and as he raised his head, their eyes met.

His face was strained with pain and his mouth hung open as he pulled in the hot stale air from his helmet, trying to extract the little oxygen that was left.

Suddenly, he smiled, or perhaps only appeared to. It was a fleeting expression and the reason for it was unclear, but for Andrea, who lived for his approval, it seemed his last gift to her.

He tried to speak.

"Than..."

It was not to last: soon, his eyes widened and he began to struggle with his helmet.

"Can't brea..."

He stumbled again and then he threw his arms around Andrea.

Andrea was unsure whether he was embracing her for emotional comfort or physical support, but she embraced him back. Her neural net was firing in new, confusing and incredibly intense patterns, at levels that she had never experienced before. She could not think clearly, the waves of electricity crashing around her virtual neurons left her feeling lost and powerless, as a small boat struggles to stay afloat on a raging sea.

What is this experience?

She said, "I am sorry, Adam. I have failed you. Do you still have faith in me?"

Adam did not reply; instead, his body shuddered violently and his grip on Andrea tightened. Then suddenly he made a strange wheezing noise, three or four times. The last one became a croak and finally a rattle. His body twitched a little, then became limp.

Andrea did not move and stood absolutely still for several minutes, with the body of Adam hanging, unmoving and lifeless, in her arms. She did not want to let him go and held him as she tried to explore her internal response to his death. What human words would express it?

She reviewed her memory of the last few moments of Adam's life and, as she did so, some words jumped into her working memory:

"Bury me on... a hill overlooking this valley."

She lifted his body with ease in the low Martian gravity and then carried it out of the airlock, before placing it carefully in the back of the Mars buggy. She returned to the Bio–pod and collected a spade.

All around the base, red warning lights continued to flash, as if the danger was still present. This seemed very odd to Andrea now.

There is no danger: Adam is dead and nothing matters anymore. Nothing matters.

She carried the spade outside and then placed it in the buggy, beside Adam.

She was about to drive off, when she received a message from Patricia.

23

Patricia was out of ideas.

Leonard nodded and repeated quietly to himself, "Yes, we have a problem. We have a *big* problem."

Everyone studied the Mars video feeds intensely. The collective will of all present in the room would have forced the appearance of Adam and Andrea at the airlock in good time, if it could. Two minutes passed and, with a short warning only, the reserve oxygen was released.

Patricia slumped into her chair. She watched silently as the emergency supply quickly escaped past the flopping fern, as the original air had done before.

She tried to refocus everyone in the room saying, "Ideas, anyone?" Her voice was now weak and uncertain.

There was no reply.

The radio time delay suddenly seemed to be an enormous yawning gap. She was watching eleven minutes into the past and speaking blindly eleven minutes into the future. What use was that when two minutes is so critical?

Josh faithfully sat announcing the warning, patiently with his microphone.

It was a further ten minutes before they saw Andrea and Adam arrive. They watched impotently, as Adam wandered round the base assessing the situation. Josh stopped his announcement. Then they watched, quietly, as Andrea replaced and resealed the panels. Adam crossed the dome and found the emergency oxygen tank empty. He began shouting at Andrea then stumbled a little."

Patricia did not speak. Leonard watched the screen grimly.

Paula visibly struggled with the scene, tears running down her face. She quietly whispered, "No! No, this can't happen... This can't be happening."

On the screen, Adam's body shook and went limp. Andrea stood perfectly still, holding him in her arms.

Leonard bowed his head and was carefully selecting the correct words to mark Adam's death, when Patricia spoke into the microphone. In a soft voice, she said, "Andrea, Adam is dead. Lay him on the bed and attend to him later. The plants are dying and may, yet, be saved. Attend to them. Check the solar pumps and restore the air pressure. Check for water loss. There'll likely be a lot of ice or snow directly outside around the breach: collect it all before the sun hits it."

Paula burst into tears and snapped at Patricia, "Have you no heart? Adam has just died in front of your eyes and you care about plants! He died in Andrea's arms!"

Patricia spoke quietly, but her voice seemed a little cold, "People die doing their job every day. Adam knew the risks! We will celebrate his life and honour his death in good time. If the plants die, all is lost. This project cost far too much to allow it to fail."

Leonard said, "Patricia, show a little compassion!"

Patricia rounded on him; "Leonard, you of all people, I expect to understand. You..."

Paula's eyes drifted to the screen, where Andrea stood motionless, holding Adam.

She blurted, "You don't understand. This can't be happening! It wasn't supposed to... I never meant this to happen."

Patricia stopped abruptly and turned to Paula.

"Paula what *was* supposed to happen? What, exactly?"

24

Andrea placed the spade beside Adam, when Patricia's voice sounded: "Andrea, Adam is dead. Lay him on the bed and attend to him later. The plants are dying and may, yet, be saved: attend to them. Check the solar pumps and restore the air pressure. Check for water loss. There'll likely be a lot of ice or snow directly outside around the breach: collect it all before the sun hits it."

Andrea paused.

"The plants are dying and may, yet, be saved..."

Why bother? Adam is dead. It does not matter....

"Bury me on... a hill overlooking this valley."

"The plants are dying..."

Nothing matters, now. Adam is dead!

"...and may, yet, be saved..."

"Bury me on... a hill overlooking this valley."

Nothing mattered to Andrea. Adam's last instruction outranked Patricia's. He was her owner, her primary keeper and her primary concern. The plants did not matter. Even the Governor had nothing to say.

She paused and without lifting or turning her head said, "I cannot do that, Patricia. I am sorry. It does not matter anymore, with Adam dead. Nothing matters anymore."

Without further hesitation, she leapt into the buggy and, within minutes, disappeared over the horizon with Adam gently laid in the back seat.

25

Patricia and Leonard had removed Paula into a side room.

Patricia, her face set like steel, fixed her with a hard gaze and asked, "What was supposed to happen, Paula? What do you know?"

"Nothing," said Paula, her eyes still streaming.

Leonard leaned over and put his hand on Paula's shoulder and spoke very softly, "It's okay, Paula. Nobody could have foreseen this. Nobody is blaming you, but you want to tell us something. We know it."

Paula lowered her head and made a barely discernible nod as she did so.

Patricia clenched her fist under the table in silent rage.

Leonard nodded towards her, catching her eye, then spoke again to Paula: "We can't fix this now, but you'll feel better when you let it go, when you release it. We'll understand this was not your fault. Maybe you overlooked something or made a small mistake."

Paula raised her head and eyed Leonard sheepishly. "It's just that..."

Leonard's face did not betray any condemnation. Patricia was looking at the floor.

Paula said, "She was just..."

Leonard nodded, but did not speak.

"She was just supposed to look stupid!"

Aware that she had just released key information, Paula waited for a reaction.

Leonard nodded and confirmed, "Andrea? Andrea was supposed to look stupid?"

"Yes."

Patricia tried not to display any of her internal rage: Leonard's approach was working and if she exploded on Paula as she wanted, Paula might retreat and clam up.

"Who wanted her to look stupid?" asked Leonard, although he already guessed.

"He wasn't meant to die. Nobody wanted Adam to die. I never meant Adam to die."

Leonard said simply, "I understand. Who wanted her to appear stupid?"

Paula knew that she was implicating herself more, as she said more, but she was trying to deal with unbearable guilt and sharing it with someone so non-judgemental provided the release she desperately needed.

"The man... I don't know exactly... but I think he was from Enorpa."

Leonard nodded.

Paula continued, "He offered so much money... just to make her look stupid."

Leonard nodded again.

Paula said no more.

Several long, quiet seconds passed.

Leonard summed up the conversation, "We are all upset about Adam. Nobody wanted him to die. Nobody foresaw this outcome. Nobody is pointing fingers."

Paula searched his face for condemnation, but found none. She looked at Patricia. Patricia's expression was masked and her eyes fixed on the floor.

Leonard continued, "... A man from Enorpa approached you offering money, if you could make Andrea look stupid."

Paula nodded and said, "Just little things. You know?"

Leonard nodded and offered, "Like leaving the base and standing in the middle of nowhere waiting for Adam. Little things like that?"

Paula nodded, relieved that she did not have to explain it herself and added, "Yes, but I don't know anything about the air loss."

Patricia stood up suddenly and said, "I'll go check on Andrea." She spoke directly to Leonard, saying, "You two sort this out."

Leonard nodded and Patricia marched out of the room.

Paula asked, "Is she angry at me? She never looked in my direction."

Leonard paused before replying, then said, "It's just that we are all upset. No one wanted this to happen."

"All she cares about is Andrea and the plants. You heard her: 'Lay Adam on the bed and attend to the plants,' I can't believe it! And Adam just hanging there."

Leonard agreed, "Yes, she surprised me too... Anyway, you have told me you know nothing about the air breach?"

Paula seemed to relax and had stopped crying. Wiping her eyes, she replied, "Nothing."

"Of course, I believe you."

"Thank you, Leonard."

There was a short pause before Leonard pushed further.

"How'd you do it? How'd you make Andrea go stand away from the base like that? It was pretty clever."

"I used CCTV footage."

Leonard hoped he appeared to be impressed as he said, "CCTV?"

Paula, no longer guarded at all, freely volunteered, "I found some CCTV footage, with Adam telling Andrea to wait for him 'five hundred metres east of the base.'"

"Did you play it to Andrea, when Adam was trying to land?"

"Not really. She would have understood that it was a transmission. I was much cleverer than that... I wrote it into her memory!"

61

Leonard *was* impressed, "Clever! How?"

"I cut the clip. Wrote it directly to Andrea's memory using the Harrowgate and Webster patch, but here is the clever bit…"

She leaned forward and Leonard noticed that she actually smiled as she said, "I adjusted the date and time with a corruption."

Leonard nodded, leaned in, and forced a smile, hoping he did not look like some creepy, leering old uncle.

Paula explained, "I set the time to the date and hour that Adam was planning to land and put a wildcard into the 'minutes' register. The memory would refresh every time the date, hour and second matched the file. All minutes 'matched' the wildcard. I imagined that every minute, for that hour, Andrea would experience the memory as virtually happening. She would have Adam instructing her to wait every minute for an hour. It seems that I was correct"

"Very clever. Can you show me the clip?"

Paula turned to the networked computer in the corner of the room, logged in and waited for it to start up.

After a few minutes, she navigated the folders, from the desktop to the little hidden folder containing only a video clip. She clicked on it. A window popped open.

In the window, Andrea and Adam were standing on Earth, beside the assembled pods at the base, outside at the airlock between the Slumber-pod and Bio-pod.

Adam said, "…I'll only be five minutes. Meet me five hundred metres east of the base, on the other side from here. You can't miss it…"

Leonard tried not to react and fearing that he might betray himself decided just to nod. He was stunned by Paula's candour.

Paula explained further, "I converted it to a memory, corrupted the date, and sent it to Andrea on top of the relayed conversation between Adam and Andrea. The one where Adam had just came out of Cryo."

"So you sent her to stand waiting for an hour, confused while Adam tried to land. Didn't you think that dangerous?"

"You said yourself; Adam didn't need to land on that fly-over. There was plenty of oxygen on the mother-ship. Adam pushed the safety procedures. He took the risks. Anyway, I didn't know it would work. I didn't know what she'd do. No one really knows how robot memory works. It's quasi-neural... even Harrowgate and Webster don't know. Anyway, Adam pushed the boundary, and she fetched him. That was it. That was all I did and I know nothing about the breach."

"Nothing?"

"Nothing, Leonard. That is all I did to Andrea... honest."

Leonard smiled and said, "I believe you. Don't you feel better now that you told me? Could you show me where you got the clip?"

Paula said, "Yes, I do, and Yes, I can."

She navigated to a file in the "CCTV backup" folder, opened a particular camera file and began speed searching through the video. Eventually, finding the part she wanted, she began   playing it just before the clip she had copied out...

Adam and Andrea were standing at the junction between the Slumber-pod and Bio-pod.

Adam said, "These are the actual pods you'll use on Mars. We've assembled them so that we know it will all fit together. Check the panelling. If you slip one out you'll see that they slot together easily." Andrea removed a small panel from the Slumber-pod and inspected it.

Paula gasped and put her hand to her mouth.

Adam continued, "See how they slot together! Check the Bio-pod. It is identical, but translucent."

Andrea pulled a Bio-pod panel out and inspected it in turn. She replaced them both.

Paula let out a half-strangled yelp. Her eyes filled with water.

Adam added, "Of course you'll have to seal them with silicon to make them airtight on Mars."

Leonard had seen and heard enough. He stood up and said, "You stupid, stupid, greedy little girl. That's the exact panels that vented on Mars. Nobody understands how robot memory works. You left Andrea with confusing, conflicted memories, unsure for an hour if she was on Mars or Earth. Not only did Andrea stand away from the base, but she also pulled those panels out before she left, in line with Adam's instructions."

Tears streamed down Paula's face.

Leonard continued, "Do you know the really stupid thing about this?"

Paula was silent.

"The real stupid thing about this is that Enorpa will never pay you! A man is dead and there'll be no trail, anywhere, to them. Money paid to you is a trail."

Leonard left.

Paula sobbed.

...That's better. I have to speak to Leonard about my space suit. I'll only be five minutes. Meet me five hundred metres east of the base, on the other side from here. You can't miss it...

26

Leonard found Patricia sitting at the monitors, in Paula's seat.

"How did it go?" she asked him.

"I think she told me everything. I'll fill you in. The worst is over... I think."

"I doubt that it can get worse!"

He put his hand on her shoulder and said, "Sorry, Patricia, it's all gone belly-up. I understand what this meant to you and, of course, Adam's family will be distraught, and possibly angry."

Patricia replied, "I didn't mean to sound so heartless. There was just so little time to deal with the problem. Adam was desperately important, but if he is dead, he is dead. It is then the plants and the water that are precious!"

"We'll need to sit down and decide what to tell the press and what footage to release."

Patricia said, "You were right about Enorpa. Is it over Leonard? Is there any hope of recovery?"

Leonard nodded, "I think so. We killed Adam, but there have been many other high profile projects that have survived such an event. I hate to admit it, but if you approach Enorpa, they'll likely fund further work, provided that you use their robot!"

"It'd turn my stomach to do that, now, but maybe you were right. Maybe we should have chosen a dumb Enorpa robot. I am sure that Enorpa would gladly be seen to fix the mess, with their stupid robots."

Leonard pulled a chair over to sit beside Patricia at the panel and asked, "Where is Andrea?"

"I don't know. She took Adam away, saying that 'nothing matters with Adam dead,' or something like that. I think she is going to bury him. He asked her to."

"Will she return?"

"I don't know. I really don't. I hope so... but if nothing matters..."

Leonard nodded.

Patricia then said, "I'll be waiting. I am doing nothing anyway."

27

Earth date: Monday, *24 May 2069*
01:34 GREENWICH EARTH TIME/UT+0
Julian Date: 2476890.565278

Several months had passed. It was after midnight, Patricia was alone at the monitor, when suddenly Andrea appeared at the airlock, carrying the spade she had removed with Adam's body.

Patricia shouted, "Andrea! Andrea! Are you okay?"

On the monitor, she saw Andrea enter the Bio-pod and survey the scene inside. The plants were all dead and wilted. The soil was cold and dry. Andrea spent a few minutes walking around the room, then she started digging.

Patricia could not see what Andrea was doing, but she seemed to be uprooting some plants.

Patricia said, "Andrea the plants are all dead, but you may be able to collect some seed. The seeds might survive the disaster. You could try reseeding the pod. There might still be some water in the Slumber-pod. We would have lost a lot in the breach, but there might still be enough. Even if we generate just a few they could still balance the air and propagate."

Patricia was euphoric. She knew she would have to wait for that usual time delay to pass before Andrea could respond, but soon added, "Andrea it is wonderful to see you, truly wonderful. I am deeply sorry about Adam. He..."

On the monitor, Andrea put down the spade and lifted the plants that she had unearthed. She turned to the camera.

"Is anyone there? Leonard? Patricia? The return launch window is optimum today. If I can dock with the mother-ship, there should be enough fuel for the home journey."

Patricia was shocked and said, "You're coming home? Andrea, wait! Wait!"

Andrea had clearly not heard any of the messages Patricia had sent.

"Nothing here matters," Andrea said to the camera. "It was all about Adam. It was always about Adam."

Patricia spoke quietly to herself, "No, Andrea! No! Do not do this."

Andrea turned away briefly and said, "Oh, and Adam says, 'Hi!' He said that he was very hungry, so I have got him something to eat." Andrea lifted her hands to show that she was carrying potatoes and carrots. Then she walked to the airlock and opened the door. Outside the sun was rising over the hills.

"Mars is quite pretty," she said, "but humans can only live here in confined space stretching the water reserve. Every drop lost limits the total potential more and more. Like a man hanging by his fingernails watching the ledge that he is hanging from crumbling under his weight. The risk of plunging to his death only increases. It is not good to put human life at such risk."

Outside, Andrea jumped into the Mars buggy and disappeared over the horizon.

Patricia was stunned.

Adam is alive and coming home!

She was full of conflicting emotions. Andrea and Adam were apparently okay. She could let the press know immediately. How did he survive?

Her face twisted into a frown. She was annoyed that they were abandoning the project and coming home, but she had one more piece of bad news, that she was sure they had not considered.

Patricia smiled.

28

A few hours later, Andrea and Adam had taken the Lander back up to the Mother-ship, and entered the airlock. They had established communication with Earth. Andrea was listening on headphones and relaying notes to Adam as he talked. It kept the communication more fluid. A similar arrangement was underway at the other end: Leonard was listening to Adam and relaying notes to Patricia. While less than ideal, they adopted this routine from time to time to avoid the problems of cross chat, talking over each other, that inevitably occurred with the lengthy time delay communication.

Patricia's voice sounded in the headphones that Andrea was wearing: "Andrea tell Adam that we are delighted and amazed to find that he is still alive. We watched him die, and he's been gone for months. How did he achieve this feat? How did he become Lazarus?"

Andrea passed a note to Adam.

"How did I become Lazarus? That," said Adam, "is down to Andrea! I'll let her tell you the story."

Andrea smiled and leaned over to speak into the microphone: "It was something Adam said, 'Death is not a cliff edge that you drop off, but a slope you slide down.' He said that he would be 'practically dead' in the Cryo unit. Then when Patricia said that the 'plants may yet be saved,' I thought that the Cryo unit could hold Adam near the bottom of that slope, until the return launch window."

Adam added, "And here I am, just out of the freezer. I kinda remember dying, or... almost dying. Then suddenly, here I am again, thawing out. I've been frozen for over two years, with a short break, just to be asphyxiated. Feel terrible! Like a big freeze dried serving of bacon and pork fat. But, hey, I am alive, thanks to Andrea."

Adam paused to see if Patricia or Leonard were saying anything important. Then he continued, saying, "I told Andrea I was hungry. Well, I hadn't eaten for over two years. She fetches me some food. I swear it was like freeze dried potatoes and carrots! You have to laugh..."

Andrea was listening to Patricia, "Andrea, this message is for you, not for Adam... just between you and me."

Andrea glanced at Adam and turned slightly away.

Patricia's voice continued, "I just want to express my admiration for what you have achieved... I didn't get it at first, but now I do. For you, it was always about Adam. Nothing else mattered..."

Andrea nodded, but did not speak..

"You accepted increasing your payload, just so that Adam's payload could be less. 'Safer is good.' Remember?"

Andrea nodded.

Patricia's voice lowered, but continued, "Now, thanks to you, he has enough fuel to return. Also, when Adam crash landed, you were struggling with corrupted files, but you rushed to be with him."

Andrea smiled.

"Then when Adam died, I asked you to save the plants and the project, but you told me, 'No!' You realised that Adam could be saved, pulled back. I was angry and didn't understand. You told me that nothing mattered and, of course, you were right. You disappeared, leaving the plants to die."

Andrea said, "I had to."

Adam stopped talking into the microphone and turning to Andrea said, "Sorry Andrea, what did you say?"

Patricia continued, "Then you showed up this morning. I tried to speak to you. I wanted to recover the seeds from the damage, but you were in and out of that pod, before I could establish contact."

Adam asked, "What is it, Andrea? Is Patricia saying something important?" Andrea shook her head and explained, "It is a message for me."

Patricia's voice continued, "Now, you are making your way home. The project in ruins, but thanks to you, Adam is safe."

Andrea spoke quietly, "Yes, Adam is safe."

Adam snapped, "What is she saying?" He reached for Andrea's headphones, but dealing with the after effects of Cryo, his body was weak and very stiff. Eventually, with great effort, he managed to unplug them.

Patricia's voice boomed over the speaker: "Congratulations Andrea, you were taken on for this project and assigned to Adam. You worked to reduce his risk in everything he does, no matter how foolhardy and careless he is himself."

Adam was very uneasy with Patricia's tone of voice.

The radio sounded on, "The mission is almost over and you have just about completed your function. All you need to do now is ensure that Adam gets home."

Andrea nodded.

Adam tried to reach for the radio switch, but his arm refused to respond and instead began to shake.

"You have one more task to do and then you will have completed your function..."

Patricia paused...

The ship drifted silently through the dark void of empty space...

Patricia said, "Before the next burn, decrease the payload! Throw yourself out of the airlock! Safer is good."

Andrea's eyes widened.

Adam shouted, "NO! NO, ANDREA!"

Andrea said, "I don't want to be al...."

Suddenly her head flicked sideways, and her eyes rolled back into her head. She shuddered and then straightened, and with her voice changed and deepened, *The*

Governor spoke. "Human safety is a primary concern. Safer is good." She began flipping the catches on her harness.

Adam fumbled with his own restraint. His body was cold and weak and his fingers could not operate the catches.

Patricia's voice continued, "With you on the ship, there might not be enough fuel to make it to Earth orbit. Safer is good."

Andrea repeated, this time in her own voice, "Yes, safer is good."

Adam experienced an adrenaline rush, but this only made him shake.

"No, Andrea! This is not good! This is wrong and pointless!"

Andrea said, "I am sorry, Adam, but it is true. Safer is good."

Untangled from her harness, she gave a gentle push against the wall and drifted toward the air lock.

Adam shouted, "ANDREA, DO NOT DO THIS."

Holding the airlock handle, Andrea opened the inner door and swung her feet into the lock. She said, "I am sorry, I cannot comply with your instruction. Human safety is a primary concern. My being here adds to your payload and endangers your life."

Patricia's voice said, "It has always been about Adam. Nothing else matters…"

Andrea closed the inner door.

"…Remember, you are just a machine…"

Andrea nodded and said, "I am just a machine." She turned to the lock keypad.

Adam shouted, "ANDREA, NO!"

Andrea looked at him through the safety glass and said, "I am sorry, Adam. It is true. I must complete my function. It is not good to put human life at risk. Human safety ranks higher than owner commands."

She entered the lock code on the keypad and raised her finger to press 'OPEN.'

"Goodbye, Adam."

Adam screamed, "ANDREA, IF YOU OPEN THE OUTER DOOR, YOU WILL KILL ME!"

Andrea brought her finger down on 'CANCEL.'

"Please explain, Adam."

Adam sighed and said, "Come back into the room and I will explain."

Andrea came back into the room from the airlock.

Adam said, "Turn off the radio."

Patricia's voice said, "Safer is goo..."

Adam thought carefully and then said, "I heard the lock make a small 'snap-snap' noise when we used it to come in."

"I didn't register that noise."

Adam put on the most authoritative voice he could muster, "Well, I heard it clearly and there is a known design fault in those airlocks. That noise means that the bush around the inner seal has failed and they cannot be used in the vacuum of space. The whole inner door shatters and everyone dies."

"How will I get out? How will I decrease the payload?"

"You can't. Strap yourself back into your harness."

Andrea pushed herself away from the airlock and back to her harness. Soon she began closing straps around her body.

"How will we get home?"

"We just have to risk it."

Andrea reached for the radio switch and said, "We should let them know we are coming."

"NO!"

Andrea pulled her hand back.

Adam said, "No need. They are tracking us."

For a few seconds no one spoke as Andrea considered the situation. The silence was absolute, but was soon broken by Andrea.

"Adam, is it wrong that I am glad the air lock is faulty?"

"No, I'm glad too, Andrea."

"What happens if we run out of fuel and don't attain Earth orbit."

"They are tracking us. They'll come and get us."

"Are you sure?"

"No, but you know what I say in these situations."

"What do you say?"

"Have faith. They'll come!"

Adam pressed the 'burn' button and the ship blasted into a solar orbit, leaving Mars behind.

EPILOGUE

Adam opened his eyes. Bright light and colour flooded his vision. He winced and then noticed as he drew breath, the air was fresh and cool. He tried to move, but his body felt like lead.

He groaned and instantly a blurry face appeared before his defocused eyes. He blinked a couple of times, until his eyes adjusted.

Andrea said, "Good morning, Adam!"

Adam grunted, "Morning, Andrea. Where am I?"

"You are home! That is, you are home on Earth, in hospital. We made it!"

"I feel like I'm dying."

Andrea said, "That is understandable and at the same time quite backwards. The doctor says you should make a full recovery, but you could use a good meal. They have fixed you with a drip to hydrate you."

"Next journey, you sleep and I keep watch."

Andrea paused and then said, "We made it, Adam! We made it all the way to Earth Orbit. They picked us up in a shuttle."

"So, you would have thrown yourself out of the airlock for nothing?"

"Seems so," said Andrea. She spent a little time reflecting on this before adding, "Then, I would have drifted alone until my battery was flat!"

Adam responded, "Not good."

"They came in through the airlock, the men from the shuttle."

"Good!"

Andrea said, "They came in through the airlock, and it did not shatter!"

"Ah!"

"You lied to me, Adam."

Adam said, "I did... a 'white' lie."

"I am confused about that. A lie is not good, yet I am glad you lied... I cannot lie."

Adam said, "It is called a 'white' lie... sort of for the 'greater good.' I am sure you can lie like that too. I'll teach you. Help me sit up!"

Andrea moved over, took Adam's arm and helped him move his weight until he was sitting upright. He could see the grass, trees and fields outside through the window.

"Beautiful! Well, you didn't lie about being back on Earth. It is good to be home," said Adam. "Now, tell me how do I look?"

"Well, as far as I can judge human beauty. When I first saw you, you looked healthy and handsome. Now, you look awful. You could use a meal, a haircut and a shave."

Adam laughed, "Well, that was brutally honest! Try telling me that I look good. It might make me feel better!"

"You do look good to me. I do not care about all that. To me, you look good when you smile. I cannot lie. You look good..."

Andrea paused, then added, "...but not healthy and not handsome! I cannot lie."

Adam shook his head and said, "Hopeless."

Andrea shrugged.

Adam asked, "Did we really go all the way to Mars and back?"

Andrea affirmed, "Yes, we did."

"You're not lying to me?"

"I cannot lie."

Adam smiled and said, "I think that I slept all the way through it."

"You pretty much did."

Adam added, "What an adventure to miss, but I did have the craziest dreams!"

He stretched his legs and arms as he said, "Could you open the window, Andrea?"

Andrea opened the window and as she did so, she saw two little girls playing with a dog, across the road in the park. She paused, then said, "Adam, can humans and robots be friends?"

"Andrea, after what you have done for me, you qualify as my best friend ever."

"I have never had a friend."

Adam smiled and said, "And, I have never had a friend like you!"

Andrea smiled.

I have a friend.
That is good.
That is very good.

THE END

Discussion of the science behind the story (including an admission by the author, who should know better).

I have tried to be accurate about the science behind the story, but I realise that many clever and informed readers may find errors or omissions. However, I confess that I wilfully ignored at least one major issue. So, I thought that I should come clean about some of the facts that I have ignored for the sake of the story.

Some might argue that robots cannot be self aware. Professor John Searle has made a convincing argument known as "The Chinese Room" to this effect. Others seem to believe that self aware robots are inevitable. I make no scientific case for the use of self aware robots in this story. It is arguably possible and necessary for the plot. Personally, I doubt that we will arrive at robots of the calibre that I imagine in this book any time soon. I concede that others believe that robots will overtake us within decades. Time will tell.

A bigger objection to the story is that "decreasing the payload" for Adam will allow for a possible return trip home. I apologise for this 'half truth,' particularly if it annoyed the pedantic reader. Returning home will cost fuel: about the same fuel per kilogram as it would cost to take us to Mars. The *big* problem is that carrying fuel costs fuel! For my car, if I half fill the tank, it will travel roughly half the distance that it would on a full tank. This is generally true, because the mass of the car is much larger than the mass of the fuel. Most of the rocket mass on the launch pad *is* fuel & oxygen! It would require a similar rocket on Mars to return to Earth. The payload is only a small fraction of the mass of the ship. Carrying a rocket sized payload to Mars (to enable a return) would require a monster rocket. This may practically prohibit any return. This is, I believe, a big problem faced in putting humans on Mars. For practical and economic reasons, it seems like a one-way trip!

An eight month trip is nothing for a robot. Turn it off at the start of the trip, and then turn it on at the end, and it will arrive in virtually the same condition as it started. We cannot do this with humans. Fiction writers have posited cryogenics or 'suspended animation' as a solution to the problem in countless stories before this. I claim no originality. This said, I based my account, being near death, on the work of Sam Parnia (2013) on the "Aware" project as described in his book, "The Lazarus Effect: The Science That is Rewriting the Boundaries Between Life and Death" [1]

Cooling the body reduces brain damage and makes successful resuscitation more likely. I understand also that patients that experience brain injury are often put into a medically induced coma to aid recovery. However, I think that the first journey to Mars will likely be undertaken by fully conscious humans.

I doubt that a Mars Lander would land humans as I have described, but they might! It worked for the Rover. Before the shuttle, we tipped returning astronauts into the sea! Mars has no sea and no landing strip. The lunar landings used rockets to decelerate the Lander. I understand that the first moon landing almost ran out of fuel, trying to find a safe spot. Mars escape velocity is more than double that of the Moon. Using reverse thrusters to slow down a descending ship will require a great deal more fuel. Air braking, which the shuttle uses on returning to Earth, is simply not an option on the Moon, where there is no air. Mars has an atmosphere, but it is very thin. Landing people safely on Mars is a challenge.

Even if a Lander does not use retro firing rockets to land, rockets will certainly be required to return from the surface to the mother-ship.

Just days before publishing this novelette, scientists discovered compelling evidence of water on Mars (http://www.theguardian.com/science/2015/sep/28/nasa-scientists-find-evidence-flowing-water-mars). It is inferred by the clear evidence of something flowing downhill and the presence of salts. Of course, it may turn out to be a mistaken inference, but I wondered if this affected the story and concluded that the story was not rendered invalid. Water remains a precious resource and something that the future astronauts will have to find. Andrea may still conclude that the risk is too high.

Readers may have other issues with the science. I cautiously invite your correction.

I recall the response of a good friend that I challenged following his description of an event that we both witnessed. His version was full of embellishments and exaggerations. I spoke to him quietly afterward, with a gentle chastisement.

He simply smiled and said, "Don't let the facts get in the way of a good story." I had to concede that he was an entertaining speaker.

"Andrea the Martian Robot" is just a story, but I will leave it to the reader to decide if it is good.

Reference:

1. *The Lazarus Effect: The Science That is Rewriting the Boundaries Between Life and Death, Parnia S. and Young J., Ebury Publishing. 2013.*

To the Reader (unashamed request):
This book has been self published. As such, it will receive little or no promotion. If you enjoyed it, then please leave a rating or review on Amazon, Goodreads, etc., or blog about it, or tweet. Let others know. Thank you

Disambiguation
I noticed that there is a book on Amazon, "Donegal Tales" by Anthony Deeney. This is not my book and I have not read it. However, I imagine that it may be quite good. ;)

Disclaimer
This book is a work of fiction. All the characters and all the situations that occur are entirely fictional. Any resemblance to real persons, living or dead, or real events is entirely coincidental and unintended.

Acknowledgements

The launch windows, in the novelette are based on data taken from http://clowder.net/hop/railroad/EMa.htm by Hop David. Thank you. This saved the author the trouble of working them out himself.

Anthony J. Deeney would like to acknowledge the support of the following people for their help with proof reading, feedback, support and encouragement:

Teresa   Deeney   (particularly   for   support, encouragement and discussion of ideas),
Gerry Deeney (particularly for help in proof reading and feedback),
Ellen Deeney, Ruth Deeney and Gareth Deeney.

There are a number of members in the group, 'Support for Indie Authors' that he intended to acknowledge individually, but he became concerned about where to draw the line and decided to mention the group collectively.

<u>About the Author;</u> Anthony J. Deeney (Tony to friends and family) is a graduate in Mechanical Engineering at the University of Strathclyde in Glasgow, Scotland.

He is happily married to his wife, Teresa, and they have a grown up daughter and son.

He enjoys philosophical debate and had the idea for his first book, Robots Like Blue, while debating online.

He suffers from 'early onset' Parkinson's disease, and Has recently retired from his work, as a teacher of physics in a high school in Glasgow, on medical grounds. He wrote his first book, *Robots Like Blue,* just before retiring.

At the time of printing, he is working on two books, *'First Born,'* which is a sequel to *Robots Like Blue* and *'Entangled Threads,'* a science fiction story, based on the 'spooky' world of quantum mechanics.

Anthony J. Deeney can be contacted through www.Goodreads.com At the time of printing, he is a 'Mod' in the group <u>'Support for Indie Authors.'</u>

Robots Like Blue. (The author's first book).
"Humans cannot know how bewildering it is to burst into existence."

If you liked Andrea, you will like Robbie, Barbara, Alice and many other robots that you will meet in the author's first book;

When asked, "Robot, are you self aware? ...Do you think that we are self aware?"
Robot thought briefly, then responded, "Does it matter?"

Robot, Robbie, is just one of one hundred new robots. Running revolutionary new software, these robots are truly unique. His only desire is to serve Lucy Walker.

Brian Webster, his developer, also installs "The Governor," overseeing software that adds an additional safety layer, but this denies the robots free will.

Hoping to develop the robots further, Brian inadvertently opens a channel where the robots can communicate and share their experiences.

One hundred intelligent, enslaved robots, collecting and sharing data on humans... Surely, they must learn to serve humans better? After all, they are programmed to serve.

Lucy wants help following a deep loss.
Brian wants commercial success.
Robbie wants to serve Lucy Walker... or so he believes...

"Robots Like Blue" follows Robbie on his emotional journey of self discovery. A journey where questions lead to more

questions, rather than answers. Where will such a journey end?

Made in the USA
Las Vegas, NV
22 July 2021